W9-CFD-210

I Am Humble

by Kirsten Chang

BLASTOFF! READERS

BELLWETHER MEDIA · MINNEAPOLIS, MN

Note to Librarians, Teachers, and Parents:

Blastoff! Readers are carefully developed by literacy experts and combine standards-based content with developmentally appropriate text.

Level 1 provides the most support through repetition of high-frequency words, light text, predictable sentence patterns, and strong visual support.

Level 2 offers early readers a bit more challenge through varied simple sentences, increased text load, and less repetition of high-frequency words.

Level 3 advances early-fluent readers toward fluency through increased text and concept load, less reliance on visuals, longer sentences, and more literary language.

Level 4 builds reading stamina by providing more text per page, increased use of punctuation, greater variation in sentence patterns, and increasingly challenging vocabulary.

Level 5 encourages children to move from "learning to read" to "reading to learn" by providing even more text, varied writing styles, and less familiar topics.

Whichever book is right for your reader, Blastoff! Readers are the perfect books to build confidence and encourage a love of reading that will last a lifetime!

This edition first published in 2020 by Bellwether Media, Inc.

No part of this publication may be reproduced in whole or in part without written permission of the publisher. For information regarding permission, write to Bellwether Media, Inc., Attention: Permissions Department, 6012 Blue Circle Drive, Minnetonka, MN 55343.

Library of Congress Cataloging-in-Publication Data

Names: Chang, Kirsten, 1991- author.
Title: I Am Humble / by Kirsten Chang.
Description: Minneapolis : Bellwether Media, 2020. | Series: Character education |
    Includes bibliographical references and index. | Audience: Ages 5-8 | Audience: Grades K-1 |
    Summary: ""Developed by literacy experts for students in kindergarten through grade three, this book
    introduces humility to young readers through leveled text and related photos"--Provided by publisher
Identifiers: LCCN 2019024638 (print) | LCCN 2019024639 (ebook) | ISBN 9781644871126 (library binding) |
    ISBN 9781618917928 (paperback) | ISBN 9781618917829 (ebook)
Subjects: LCSH: Humility--Juvenile literature.
Classification: LCC BJ1533.H93 C43 2020 (print) | LCC BJ1533.H93 (ebook) | DDC 179/.9--dc23
LC record available at https://lccn.loc.gov/2019024638
LC ebook record available at https://lccn.loc.gov/2019024639

Editor: Christina Leaf   Designer: Jeffrey Kollock

Printed in the United States of America, North Mankato, MN.

Table of Contents

What Is Humility?

Your soccer team wins the game. You are so happy!

5

Do you **brag** when you win? Or are you humble?

Humble people are **modest**. They do not have too much **pride**.

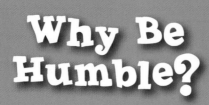

Why Be Humble?

Humble people think about how others feel.

It is okay to be proud of things you have done. But you must also be **respectful**.

People might feel bad if you act like you are better than them.

Who Is Humble?

You Are Humble!

You can be humble! When Jon makes a mistake, he says sorry.

Anna is **grateful** when she gets a gift. She says thank you!

When friends help Nic, he gives them **credit**. How will you be humble?

21

Glossary

brag

to talk too proudly about yourself

modest

does not want to talk about themselves too much

credit

praise given to someone for something they did

pride

a feeling of worth and accomplishment

grateful

thankful

respectful

showing that you honor something

To Learn More

AT THE LIBRARY

Fretland VanVoorst, Jenny. *I Am a Good Citizen*. Minneapolis, Minn.: Bellwether Media, 2019.

Kramer, Barbara. *Mother Teresa*. Washington, D.C.: National Geographic, 2019.

Murphy, Frank. *Stand Up for Sportsmanship*. Ann Arbor, Mich.: Cherry Lake Publishing, 2019.

ON THE WEB

FACTSURFER

Factsurfer.com gives you a safe, fun way to find more information.

1. Go to www.factsurfer.com.

2. Enter "humble" into the search box and click 🔍.

3. Select your book cover to see a list of related web sites.

Index

The images in this book are reproduced through the courtesy of: fizkes, front cover; Paolo Bona, pp. 4-5, 6-7;
GCShutter, pp. 8-9; wavebreakmedia, pp. 10-11, 22 (pride, respectful); CasarsaGuru, pp. 12-13; LightField
Studios, pp. 14-15; EvgeniiAnd, p. 15 (bottom left; bottom right); Feverpitched, pp. 16-17; Monkey Business
Images, pp. 18-19; Syda Productions, pp. 20-21, 22 (grateful); mediaphotos, p. 22 (brag); SolStock, p. 22
(credit); Sladic, p. 22 (modest).